SPORTS DAY

Last Day at School

By Morgan McCubbin

SPORTS DAY: *Last Day at School*

Published by
Script of Virtue Collections
https://scriptofvirtue.business.site

Written by Morgan McCubbin

Illustrated by
Freepix.com

Edited by Script of Virtue Collections

Printed by Amazon.com

DEDICATION

This book is dedicated to my teachers
of the Watford Hill Primary and Infant School;
Ms Lawrence and Ms Jarrett.

It was a day at school.

Our principal said the next day was going to be Sports Day.

Everyone was very happy.

The next day,
Sports Day finally came.
My mother, my sister and me,
arrived at school.
There was so much excitement.
Children were playing
everywhere.

When I looked around, I saw vendors selling on the left side of the road.

Some children were in their PE clothes, and some in their cheer-leading clothes.

We started the day with a
cross-country race.
Then after,
we did the regular races
on the football field.

START

Some House did the Wheelbarrow Race,

Thug-A-War, and the Sack Race.

Green House won the Sack Race.

And Blue House won the others.
My house was the Blue House.

Many children participated in the races.

Both big and small.

They all ran for hours.

3
2
1

After the games,
we all had lunch.

Everyone sat in their favourite
seats.

The vendors were very happy
to support our school's Sport Day.

After lunch,

they announced the winner.

Surprisingly, Blue House won the competition.

They had the most scores.

We were extremely happy,

but some were very sad.

Sports Day was really fun. It taught us a lot of physical activities.

The End.

www.ingramcontent.com/pod-product-compliance
Lightning Source LLC
Chambersburg PA
CBHW042130110726
48006CB00003B/828

* 9 7 9 8 8 4 6 3 2 9 7 5 1 *